W9-CIF-355

R03105 52442

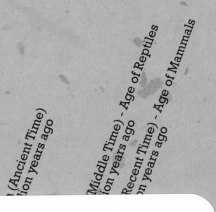

(Ancient Time)
ion years ago

(Middle Time) - Age of Reptiles
ion years ago

Recent Time) - Age of Mammals
on years ago

DATE DUE		

Cretaceous Period (140-65 mya)

ORNITHOMIMUS

Discoveries in Palaeontology

ORNITHOMIMUS

Pursuing the Bird-Mimic Dinosaur

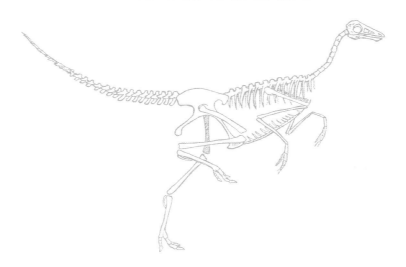

MONIQUE KEIRAN

ROYAL TYRRELL MUSEUM

RAINCOAST BOOKS

Vancouver

First published in 2001 by
Raincoast Books
9050 Shaughnessy Street
Vancouver, British Columbia
Canada V6P 6E5
www.raincoast.com

1 2 3 4 5 6 7 8 9 10

National Library of Canada Cataloguing in Publication Data

Keiran, Monique.
  Ornithomimus
(Discoveries in palaeontology, ISSN 1489-7784; no. 2)

  ISBN 1-55192-348-3

  1. Ornithomimus. 2. Paleontology—Alberta. I. Title. II. Series.
QE862.S3K46 2001   567.914   C2001-910224-0

Cover photography by Merle Prosofsky
Cover image digital manipulation by Les Smith
Cover and interior design by Gabi Proctor/DesignGeist

Raincoast Books gratefully acknowledges the support of the Government of Canada, through the Book Publishing Industry Development Program, the Canada Council for the Arts, and the Department of Canadian Heritage. We also acknowledge the assistance of the Province of British Columbia, through the British Columbia Arts Council.

Acknowledgements

Thanks to Bruce Naylor, David Eberth, Marty Hickie, Paul Johnston, Andy Neuman, Dennis Braman, Clive Coy, Philip Currie, Eva Koppelhus, Stewart Wright, Darren Tanke, Don Brinkman, Kevin Aulenback, Paul McNeil, Ruth Stockey (University of Alberta), Matt Vickaryous, Michael Ryan, Scott Mair, Julia Sankey, John Ford, Jim McCabe, Javier Palomino, Kathryn Valentine, Jackie Wilke, Vien Lam, Warren Nicholls, Betsy Nicholls, Sue Sommerville ... and many others

Photos: Dennis Braman, Don Brinkman, Clive Coy (page 32 top left and bottom), Phil Currie, Monique Keiran, O. Louis Mazzatenta (page 44 top), Monica Nash, Merle Prosofsky (pages 36 left, 38, 40, 42 left, 43, 47), Donna Sloane, Ruth Stockey (page 11), Stewart E. Wright (pages 7, 8, 10, 12, 26 top and bottom left and right, 32 right, 55 right)

Scientific advisors: Dr. Dennis Braman (Palaeobotany/Palynology), Dr. Don Brinkman (Vertebrate Palaeontology), Dr. Philip Currie (Dinosaur Palaeontology), Dr. David Eberth (Sedimentary Geology), Dr. Bruce Naylor (Vertebrate Palaeontology)

Illustrations: Melanie Ford Wilson

Special thanks to Raincoast Books, Museums Alberta and the Alberta Foundation for the Arts

The 1995 *Ornithomimus edmontonensis* was discovered by Jean Thompson and Kevin Aulenback. It was collected by Philip Currie, Clive Coy, Evan Fietz, Don Henderson, Ken Kucher and Stewart Wright. Thanks to these individuals for sharing their stories and information.

The plants, dinosaurs and other animals illustrated in this book reflect the fossil record of Dinosaur Provincial Park, Alberta. Stories and illustrations have been reviewed and approved by scientists at the Royal Tyrrell Museum of Palaeontology.

Articulated dinosaur skeletons are usually found preserved in tight, backward arches. This position is called the death pose.

The image of the *Ornithomimus* on the cover has been digitally manipulated to reflect how the skeleton would have appeared before the animal's death. In the gallery of the Royal Tyrrell Museum of Palaeontology, the specimen is in its natural death-pose position.

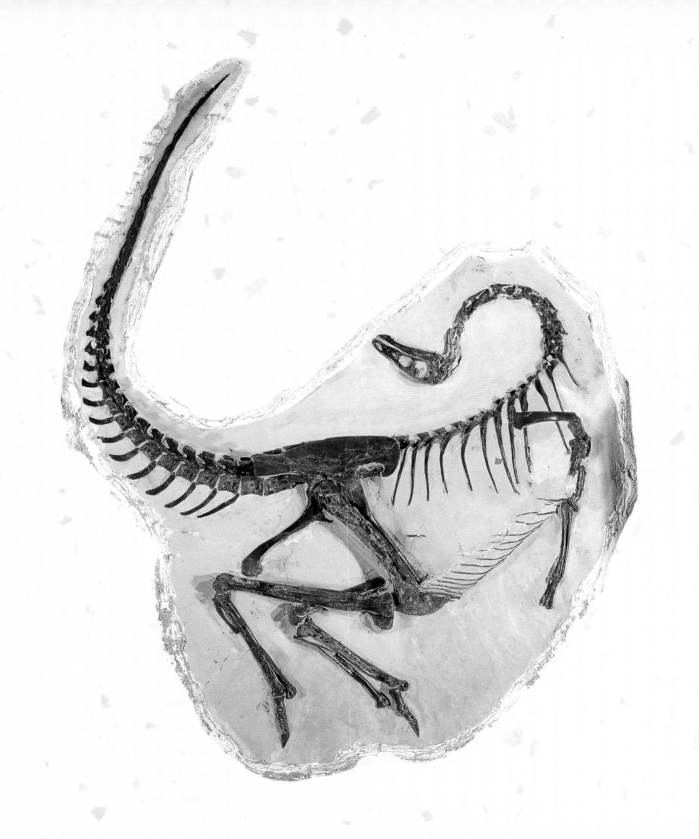

Contents

1. Discovery

Dinosaur Fossil Grounds

Dinosaur Provincial Park is so rich in **fossils** that in some places a person cannot walk without stepping on dinosaur bones.

With every rainfall and snowmelt, the remains of ancient animals are brought to light in the badlands that twist through Alberta's Red Deer River valley. The 76-million-year-old fossils emerge from hills and coulees as the ground is washed away.

Every year, scientists discover and collect **specimens** in the park that are the envy of museums and research facilities around the world.

With every rainfall, dinosaur bones emerge from the hillsides and coulees of Dinosaur Provincial Park.

Dinosaur Provincial Park is famous for fossils of dinosaurs that lived 74 to 76 million years ago, during the Late **Cretaceous** period. More than 40 dinosaur **species** have been discovered there in the 100 years since **palaeontologists** first came to the area. Of these discoveries, almost 500 are complete or nearly complete skeletons. This is an astonishing number — most dinosaur fossils found elsewhere are single bones, parts of bones or jumbled bones of many animals.

Because of the variety, number and quality of preservation of bones found there, many palaeontologists believe the park to be the best dinosaur-fossil site in the world.

However, Dinosaur Provincial Park, so rich in dinosaur bones, is poor in other fossils. It has scant record of what many dinosaurs ate. Plant fossils such as leaves, seeds and twigs are rare in the park, the result of an environment that did not preserve delicate plant material, but protected heavier, more durable bones.

The park is especially poor in fossils of flowering plants.

That's why Kirk Johnson's discovery one summer day in 1993 is all the more amazing.

A plant palaeontologist from Colorado's Denver Museum of Natural History, Johnson was hiking through the park as part of a field tour. From the road that winds through the park's restricted zone, he recognized a layer of greenish grey rock in a nearby hill. In the badlands of Montana where he spends summers collecting plant fossils, this kind of shale often contains remains of ancient plants.

Curious to see if this was the case in Dinosaur Provincial Park, Johnson investigated.

In the rocky hillside, as expected, he discovered the fossil of a single, perfect leaf from a plant that had grown and flowered there 76 million years ago.

He dug into the hillside. Impressions of gingko leaves, sycamore leaves and even fossilized seeds came to light.

Prompted by Johnson's discovery, palaeontologist Dennis Braman surveyed the site further. Braman is curator of ancient plants at the Royal Tyrrell Museum of Palaeontology, located 80 kilometres upriver in Drumheller, Alberta, and home to many of the fossils discovered in the park. He found a treasure trove of plant fossils. Their abundance and preservation promised discovery of previously unknown kinds of Late Cretaceous flowering plants, as well as extraordinary display specimens for the museum.

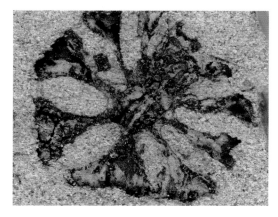

Johnson (left) and Braman found many leaf impressions of Late Cretaceous flowering plants (top left) in the fossil bed, as well as remains of other kinds of plants, such as ginkoes (top right) and sequoia-like conifers (fossil of cone, bottom right).

Ancient Worlds Beneath Our Feet

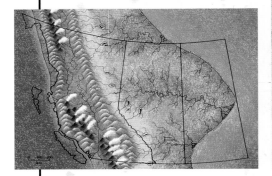

Drifting continents, receding sea levels and four recurring ice ages have changed the look of western North America in the 75 million years since dinosaurs lived here.

French explorers travelling through South Dakota in the 18th century called the twisting, eroded landscape of the region's river valleys *les mauvaises terres à traverser* — bad lands to travel through — leading to today's term "badlands."

Today's landscapes are built on the remains of ancient environments. Dinosaur Provincial Park is made of remnants of a vast, 74-million- to 76-million-year-old coastal plain. As sand, silt and mud washed down from western highlands toward the sea, layers of **sediment** formed and reformed on the plain, covering and uncovering bodies of dead dinosaurs, tree trunks and other debris. Millions of years passed and hundreds of metres of sedi-ment piled up, pressing down to turn the layers into the sandstone, siltstone and mud-stone we see today.

Cut and eroded by water and wind, the rocks provide scientists with a picture of what the area was like when dinosaurs made their homes there.

Soils made of ancient sedi-ments supported complex systems of life. Stands of trees sheltering ferns, horse-tails and early flowering plants dotted a warm, temperate landscape of marshes, streams and open plains. There were only two seasons in a year — hot and humid, and cool and drier.

Flying reptiles and **birds** nested in trees or hid in bushes. Small **mammals** scurried about, searching for seeds, fruits and insects. Turtles and crocodiles lived along the banks of streams and ponds.

This was the dinosaurs' world. Horned and duck-billed dinosaurs grazed and browsed on plants, watching for hungry **tyrannosaurs** [tigh-RAN-oh-sors]. Smaller dinosaurs such as *Troodon* [TROH-oh-don], *Dromaeosaurus* [DROH-mee-oh-SOR-us] and *Ornithomimus* [orn-ITH-oh-MIGH-mus] hunted smaller **prey**. Armoured **ankylosaurs** (an-KIGH-loh-sors) kept to high ground.

We know these animals once lived in the park because we find their teeth and bones in the rocks that form its hills and valley walls. We know the area supported diverse and abundant plant life because the animals could not have survived without plants to feed on or to find shelter among. Evidence comes from a coal seam found near the top of the valley walls, from petrified wood entombed in the rock, and from the fossil **pollens** and **spores** that Dennis Braman, **palynologist** at the Royal Tyrrell Museum of Palaeontology, isolates from the park's sediments.

Braman has found approximately 300 kinds of these tiny fossils. Only 50 of them can be linked to modern plant families, leaving scientists searching for other ways to identify the plants. Often, the only way to establish exactly what plants existed in a place millions of years ago is to find their fossilized leaves, needles, seeds and twigs.

The discovery on the hillside in Dinosaur Provincial Park was significant — it could provide important new information about the different environments in which Alberta's dinosaurs lived.

Pollens and spores are tiny capsules of genetic information plants make and use to reproduce. They are almost indestructible in environments such as rivers, streams and swamps: their outer casings are fortresses against time, water and the pressure of millions of tonnes of rock. By analyzing small samples of sedimentary rocks, Braman (below) can identify thousands of fossilized pollens and spores.

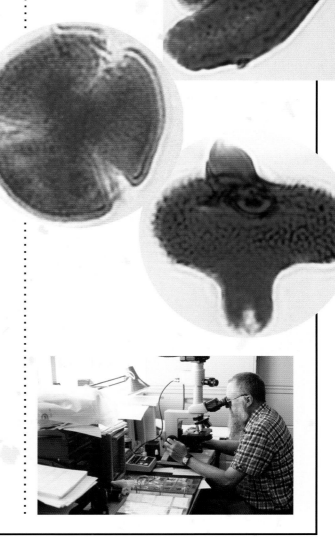

Bird-Mimic Chronicles:
Hunting

The clamour of just-awakened birds announced the coming day. As the sky paled, hundreds of birds darted through the air, their wing beats flashing on the pond's silver surface.

At daybreak, land, sky and water came alive.

The young dinosaur snapped at a passing fly and halted, listening for threatening sounds and watching for danger in the half-light. Although almost full-grown, it was the first time he had ventured so far from his family. He resumed picking his way through the horsetails and ferns toward the pond's edge, planting each step carefully and quietly.

Rings of ripples shivered across the water where fish surfaced to harvest the early-morning flurry of insects.

A sudden shaking in the brush caught the dinosaur's attention. He froze. The movement stopped. Alert, he watched, slowly extending his long neck toward it.

There, again. Something was darting through the ferns and horsetails — something small and quick. Plant stems rustled against each other, then stopped.

The dinosaur pinpointed the spot. He tensed and crouched close to the ground, watching, waiting, listening …

There! A tiny quivering, right there! In a lightning-quick burst, the young dinosaur pounced, slamming his long, three-fingered hands onto the ground where the animal should be.

Almost! His fingers brushed a tiny, furred, fleeing leg. The dinosaur gave chase, jabbing at the creature with hungry mouth and hands. His jaws snapped, but again he missed, feeling the skinny tail flick his chin as the animal disappeared down a hole and into the damp soil.

The young dinosaur slid to a stop. Head cocked, he peered through the ferns at the hole, trying to see the snack hiding within. Frustrated, he poked at the tiny hole with his long, straight claws; he rarely caught these creatures — time and again, they dashed down holes or into tangled undergrowth out of his reach.

A soft squawk sounded behind him. Turning, he saw his sister approach, her hide gleaming in the growing light. He bobbed his head at her and, leaving his unreachable prey, resumed his careful approach to the pond. Together, they trod the muddy, weed-covered shore, peering into the water for frogs or small fish to grab and gulp down.

A light, early-morning breeze sprang up, wafting across the water toward them. A gnarled log drifted slowly from the far edge of the pond.

Splashing into the shallow water, his sister thrust her head in and pulled out the limp body of a dead fish caught among the floating plants near the bank. The young dinosaur tried to grab it from her. Swiping him with her claws, she stumbled into deeper water. The young dinosaur started after.

Suddenly, the drifting "log" rose out of the water and lunged at the female, jaws wide.

She shrieked, dropping the fish. The jaws of the crocodile snapped around her small body, and she disappeared under the thrashing water, her cries drowned in blood, foam and bubbles.

The young dinosaur leapt up the bank, calling in alarm.

Perched on the side of the hill, 100 metres above the valley floor, the crew had to dig through four metres of rock to get to the layer containing the plant fossils.

July 1995

Before Braman and his field crew could collect the plant fossils, the hillside above the layer of rock in which the leaves were preserved had to be removed. Technicians Kevin Aulenback and Jean Thompson hauled a jackhammer to the site and began cutting into the hill.

It took three long, hard days of digging and shovelling for Braman and the technicians to remove rock down to a level near the plant impressions.

Early on the fourth morning — July 12 — Aulenback was operating the jackhammer. Suddenly, Thompson noticed brown dust spilling out of the hole around the jackhammer bit.

She grabbed a rock fragment, looked at it, and then jumped up.

"Kevin! Stop!" she shouted. "Bone! You're hitting dinosaur bone!"

Aulenback stopped the jackhammer, and silence descended on the **quarry**.

"You're hitting dinosaur bone!"

He bent down to examine a rock slab that had broken loose.

Sticking out of two sides were pieces of the neck bones of a small **theropod** — a hollow-boned, meat-eating dinosaur.

"Oops. It's **articulated.**"

Articulated dinosaur skeletons — skeletons with the bones positioned as they had been when the animal was alive — are rare. Articulated skeletons of theropods are almost never found.

Finding Dinosaurs

Palaeontologists search for new specimens by looking for fossils sticking out of the ground and for bone fragments washed short distances by rainfall. Trails of fragments are followed back to their sources.

By assessing what part of a skeleton is exposed and how it lies in the rock, palaeontologists estimate how much more may be present.

Sometimes, fossil exposures lead to little. Sometimes, they lead to parts of skeletons. Very rarely, they are the first bones of complete, articulated skeletons that are found.

Dinosaur Provincial Park is famous for complete, articulated dinosaur skeletons, but, even there, fewer than 500 such fossils have been discovered in the past century.

The fossil bones pierced by Aulenback's jackhammer included the neck and shoulder bones of a small, meat-eating dinosaur. With more of the dinosaur's skeleton likely hidden in the rock, the crew had to determine if more of the hillside had to be removed for the fossil to be collected.

2. Excavation

The Discovery

Word quickly spread among staff working in the park. When palaeontologist Philip Currie arrived at the plant site, rocks containing bone had been collected and placed at the side of the quarry. They included shoulder and neck bones of what looked like an **ornithomimid** [orn-ITH-oh-MIGH-mid], a small, toothless theropod dinosaur that resembled an ostrich.

Currie examined exposed ends of bones still buried. Braman and his technicians worked around him, trying to save plant fossils;

compared to an articulated theropod skeleton, fossils of plants are considered less important.

Currie roped off the corner of the quarry where the bones had been found. He and two other technicians spent the rest of the day searching for broken dinosaur fossils and trying to determine how much of the skeleton was hidden in the rock.

Ornithomimid Family Tree

Tyrannosaurs may have been the big **predators** of Late Cretaceous North America, but the group of dinosaurs believed to be among their closest relatives were small and toothless.

These dinosaurs are ornithomimids. Well-named (ornithomimid means "bird mimic"), they resembled ostriches in size and body shape — ostriches with long, stiff tails and long, thin arms. As one of the few types of theropod dinosaurs believed to have evolved away from eating only meat, ornithomimids gave up teeth, heavy bones and size for lightness and speed.

True to their name, they share many features with modern birds, and are part of the line of dinosaurs believed to have given rise to birds.

- In Alberta, three kinds of bird-mimic dinosaurs are known — *Ornithomimus*, **Dromiceiomimus** [DROH-mee-see-oh-MIGH-mus] or Emu-mimic, and **Struthiomimus** [STRU-thee-oh-MIGH-mus], Ostrich-mimic. The specimen found in Dinosaur Provincial Park in 1995 is **Ornithomimus edmontonensis** [ed-MON-ton-EN-sis].

- Early ornithomimids were about the size of a full-grown man — about two metres high and three metres from head to tail. Later bird-mimics, however, could be much larger — a partial skeleton discovered in central Alberta in 1998 measures three metres high at the hips.

- Fossils of bird-mimic dinosaurs are found throughout the northern hemisphere and possibly in Australia. It is unclear where and when they originated before they spread across the continents. All ornithomimid remains are found in Cretaceous-aged sediments, but some disputed specimens date to the **Triassic period**.

- Because of their place in the dinosaur family tree, ornithomimids are one of the most intriguing kinds of dinosaurs. Not only are they cousins to tyrannosaurs, but they may be cousins to *Troodon* — a small, large-brained theropod that never lost its taste for meat. These theories of relationships are based on skeletal comparisons — such as whether bones in the dinosaurs' wrists are **fused**, or whether the size and development of the parts of their skulls that contained their brains are similar.

- All ornithomimids had long necks, long legs, long tails, long arms and three-fingered hands with long, straight claws.

- Most ornithomimid species were toothless, relying on beaks to manipulate and tear food. Toothed ornithomimids *Harpymimus* [HAR-pee-MIGH-mus], from Mongolia, and *Pelecanimimus* [PEH-leh-KAN-i-MIGH-mus], from Spain, are believed to be early, primitive members of this dinosaur family.

Bird-Mimic Chronicles:
Hunted

Late one afternoon *during the season of long rains, the young Ornithomimus and his family paused in their search for food, their attention caught by the sound of raucous squabbling carried on gusts of wind. Through the mist and the rain, they tracked the noise to a flock of small, dark birds circling and diving behind a low rise.*

The youngsters shifted uneasily, twitching as raindrops struck their backs. In the long months since leaving the rookery where they had hatched, many had fallen to predators such as the crocodile that had killed the Ornithomimus's sister. Where once there had been 12 siblings, now only four survived. The youngsters had learned caution, and were quick to use their long legs to speed them away from danger.

However, a flock of feeding birds might mean a meal nearby; they often scavenged dead animals. The ornithomimids couldn't afford to pass up easy meat; the chill that came with the wet could be fought off only with constant feeding.

But these birds could also mean scavenging predators — ones with teeth and claws who hunted ornithomimids.

Curious and hungry, but cautious, the family started toward the commo-tion, pausing often to study the area, ready to run if threatened.

*Cresting the hill, they saw the body of a horned dinosaur — one of the great beasts whose winter herds had thundered across the ornithomimids' territory at the start of the rainy sea-son, trampling everything in their path. This one had been injured, its sides gored with deep wounds. Clearly, it had died recently; only birds had picked at it. Perhaps the rain had contained the smell of rotting flesh and kept it from attracting other **scavengers**.*

One of the young brothers started forward, curious. An angry hiss from the father cowed him back.

The ornithomimids scanned the area, watching and listening for preda-tors. Cautiously, the parents led the way to the carcass, sending birds wheeling upward in angry, squawking flight. One fluttered down and landed on the long nose horn. Eyeing the ornithomimids, it boldly hopped to the face and pecked at the hole that had contained one of the dinosaur's eyes.

Taking heart, the young Ornithomimus darted in and nipped the dinosaur's flank. Nothing happened. Growing bold, he found a strip of meat hanging loose from the animal's body and bit it off, gulping it down.

The family crowded closer, the father snapping at the bird, making it leap into the air. The ornithomimids began to feed, hissing and lunging at their feathered cousins whenever one settled near.

*Suddenly, the birds wheeled up again. The young Ornithomimus looked up. Racing toward them was a pack of sickle-clawed **dromaeosaurs**, drawn, as his family had been, by the circling birds.*

Crying alarm, the young dinosaur turned and fled, his siblings and parents close on his heels.

The dromaeosaurs marked the running dinosaurs: instinct took over — instead of stopping at the carcass, the predators gave chase, picking up speed, leaping and snapping at the tails of the fleeing ornithomimids.

Terrified, the young Ornithomimus extended his body in full flight. His long legs stretched and pumped beneath him, reaching for greater speed to escape the predators; his feet and ankles absorbed the impact of his stride, increasing his pace. Heart pounding and lungs panting, he ran faster than he had ever run before. His brother overtook him and sped past; then a sister …

They ran, flowing as a group along the curve of the land, leaping over gullies, bounding through streams, swinging around thick groves of trees. The dromaeosaurs dropped back, unable to gain on the speedy prey. When they had left the predators behind, the ornithomimids slowed, gradually coming to a stop.

Odds against Preservation

A very small number of plants and animals win the fossilization lottery. Specific conditions must occur for an organism's remains to be preserved — heavy layers of sediment to cover the body soon after death, and lack of disturbance of the sediments and the bones.

Other factors, called preservation biases, affect the odds of fossilization:

- ABUNDANCE. If there are many individuals in a species, the likelihood is greater that one will die where and when conditions for preservation are right.

- HABITAT. Species that make their homes in mountains or badlands, where **erosion** rates are high, are less likely to encounter ideal preservation conditions than species that inhabit places with high sedimentation, such as river mouths and coastal plains.

- SIZE AND DENSITY. Big, heavy bones are less likely to be washed away, weathered or crushed.

   Soft body parts, such as cartilage and muscle, and plant material, such as leaves, flowers and twigs, seldom fossilize. They usually rot away before preservation can occur. Very rarely, an animal or plant is buried in an environment where decay is slowed, and the specimen, or its presence, fossilizes. A renowned site for soft-tissue fossilization is the Burgess Shale, a mountaintop quarry in Canada's Rocky Mountains where the remnants of 505-million-year-old worms, sponges and other creatures are preserved in rock.

   Dinosaur skin impressions are another form of soft-tissue fossilization, as are the feather impressions found with fossil bird and dinosaur skeletons in northern China.

- RAPIDITY OF BURIAL. The sooner after death and the more completely an organism is buried, the less chance it will be torn apart by animals, weather or water. The remains must stay buried, as any exposure will lead to wear.

- MINERAL-RICH GROUNDWATER. When bone or wood is buried, groundwater minerals may fill their tiny holes and cracks, and strengthen them. This fossilization process is called **permineralization**. It complements **replacement**, the process by which **organic** compounds in the specimen are replaced over time by inorganic minerals.

Ornithomimid bones are extremely fragile. The bones at the front of ornithomimid skulls are less than one millimetre thick, and in some cases are thinner than a sheet of paper. The odds against intact preservation of these bones are huge.

WHEEL OF PRESERVATION

fossilization

Collection

Within days, technicians found one of the dinosaur's shin bones, a foot bone and more neck **vertebrae**. The specimen was lying in white, fine-grained sandstone immediately above the green-grey mudstone containing the fossil plants. Contact between the fossils was so close, ancient leaves were deformed under the bones.

The top of the ornithomimid's pelvis jutted above the level of the rest of the skeleton; the crew followed it to locate the tail.

It was discovered that, before the animal had been buried 76 million years before, water had washed away foot and leg bones, one hand and part of its arm. The crew widened its search, hoping to find the missing fossils nearby. Clive Coy, the technician overseeing the excavation, discovered an ornithomimid leg bone four metres north of the specimen, at the edge of the cut into the looming hill. With it was a finger bone.

The other bones weren't found. Perhaps they are lying farther into the hill, under the tonnes of rock that had not been cleared away ... Perhaps they had been washed farther away those millions of years ago ...

Coy (top left) and the crew used the dinosaur's pelvis as a starting point to find the animal's tail (top) and the outline of its body.

Beasts of a Feather

All animals, including people, have unique sets of characteristics that allow them to do some things better than others. Individual animals with the abilities and traits that enable them to better survive and reproduce pass those characteristics on to their offspring. Those that lack the necessary traits don't survive or don't reproduce as often. Over time, subsequent generations inherit fewer less-beneficial traits, while survival-enhancing characteristics become more prevalent.

Eventually, the characteristics found in the most reproductively successful animals become the most common characteristics within the population. This gradual natural selection of traits and abilities leads to the development of new species over time.

Survival of the reproductively fittest is a cornerstone of 19th-century British scientist Charles Darwin's theory of evolution by natural selection.

Darwin spent years in the South Pacific studying the region's plants and animals. His observations of those creatures led to his forming the theory published in 1859 in his book *On the Origin of Species*. Its publication loosed a scientific, social and religious storm within Victorian society as people faced the possibility that their ancestors included some very intelligent, very capable apes.

The theory bore one weakness, however: lack of specimens with physical traits halfway between groups of animals. Darwin was confident these creatures with skeletons marking transition from one kind of animal into another existed — they simply had not yet been discovered.

Three years after Darwin's theory was published, **Archaeopteryx** [AR-kee-OP-ter-iks] was described. Nineteenth-century biologist Thomas Huxley was friend and colleague to Darwin and a vocal champion of his theory. Huxley embraced *Archaeopteryx* as proof that birds evolved from dinosaurs. Clearly a bird with well-developed feathers, *Archaeopteryx* had many dinosaur-like traits — teeth, a long, bony tail and separate, clawed fingers.

However, when the 20th century arrived, Huxley's birds-from-dinosaurs theory lost favour and was largely forgotten.

Then, in 1972, John Ostrom, a palaeontologist at the Yale Peabody Museum in

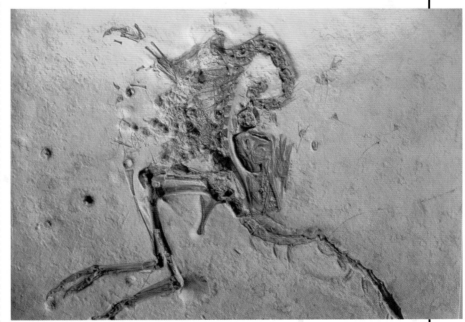

With no feather impressions preserved, the skeletons of *Archaeopteryx* (top) and *Compsognathus* (bottom) — one a bird, the other a dinosaur — are almost identical. The similarities fooled early palaeontologists enough to misidentify two specimens of the primitive Jurassic bird.

Connecticut, described the dromaeosaur **Deinonychus** [digh-NO-ni-kus]. In studying fossils of this dinosaur, Ostrom identified more than 60 skeletal features that only *Deinonychus* and modern birds share. When two animals have skeletal traits in common with each other and none other, it is evidence for evolutionary relationship. With evidence of 60 shared features to support his theory, Ostrom proposed that birds evolved from dromaeosaurs.

Archaeopteryx further convinced him. When he studied fossils of this primitive bird, Ostrom recognized two additional *Archaeopteryx* specimens that, years before, had been misidentified as chicken-sized, meat-eating dinosaur **Compsognathus** [KOMP-sog-NAY-thus].

Since then, palaeontologists have identified more than 125 features common only to theropods and birds.

Questions remained: If small, meat-eating dinosaurs are closely related to birds, where are dinosaurs' wishbones? Where are their feathers? Both are characteristics of birds. Surely, if birds evolved from dinosaurs, wishbones and feathers in dinosaur fossils would be preserved.

In 1977, scientists identified a wishbone on theropod **Oviraptor** [OH-vee-RAP-ter].

This discovery prompted researchers around the world to re-examine dinosaur fossils in their collections. Many theropod dinosaurs, including tyrannosaurs and dromaeosaurs, were found to have wishbones after all — they simply hadn't been recognized.

In 1996, dinosaur fossils with feather impressions were discovered in China. **Caudipteryx** [KAW-dee-TAIR-iks] and **Protarchaeopteryx** [proh-TAR-kee-OP-ter-ix] have well-developed feathers. **Sinosauropteryx** [SIGN-oh-sor-OP-ter-iks], the earliest of the known feathered dinosaurs, appears to have had a covering of down. In 1998, **Sinornithosaurus** [SIGN-or-NITH-oh-SOR-us] was found, complete with large, sickle-shaped claws on the hind feet, making it the first-known dromaeosaur with feathers.

Specimens of feathered dinosaurs and primitive birds continue to be discovered, each providing more information on the close evolutionary relationship between birds and dinosaurs.

Key Physical Characteristics Common to Birds and Meat-Eating Dinosaurs

- *Identical ankles with fused ankle bones*
- *Bipedality — birds and theropods had no choice but to walk only on their hind legs*
- *Almost identical hips*
- *Long, thin, spatula-shaped shoulder blades*
- *Three-fingered hands — the middle finger being the longest*
- *Hollow, thin-walled bones*
- *Similar feet — three forward-pointing toes and a big toe that points to the side or the rear*
- *Wishbones*
- *Swivelling, pulley-like wrists*
- *Feathers*
- *Similarly developed brains*

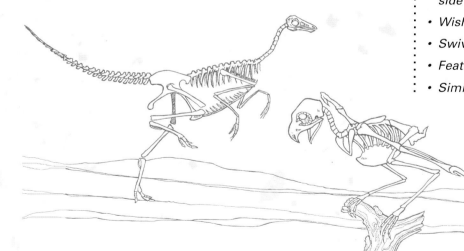

Collecting Fossils

Field crews begin collecting fossils by removing overlying rock with picks, shovels and jackhammers. Once the **overburden** is gone, crews use awls, dental picks and paintbrushes to uncover enough of the specimen to determine its outline. Little is exposed in the field where weather, accidents and even vandalism can damage uncovered fossils.

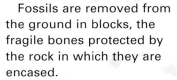

Palaeontologists measure and map how dinosaur bones are positioned in relation to each other and the type and age of rock in which they are found. Scientists analyze this information to determine what happened to the animal when it died and how it was preserved, increasing scientists' understanding of the animal and its ancient environment.

Fossils are removed from the ground in blocks, the fragile bones protected by the rock in which they are encased.

Crews **trench** around the specimen, gradually undercutting it. As they dig, they jacket the blocks with tissue and layers of burlap and plaster. Similar to the cast a doctor wraps around a broken leg, a **field jacket** keeps fossils from moving or breaking and protects them during transport. The number of layers of burlap and plaster in a jacket depends on the specimen — the bigger or more fragile the block to be removed, the thicker the jacket. In large fossil blocks, timbers strengthen and stabilize field jackets.

Eventually each block of rock, fossil, plaster and burlap sits on a small pillar like a giant mushroom. Crews flip it over and jacket the underside.

The biggest evolution in fossil collection has occurred in transportation. As late as the 1940s, horses were used to drag fossil-filled wagons through the badlands. Now, palaeontologists use all-terrain vehicles to supplement the strength and endurance of field crews. In areas that are distant or difficult to reach, helicopters deliver supplies and remove specimens.

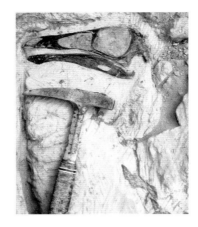

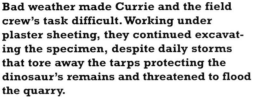

Bad weather made Currie and the field crew's task difficult. Working under plaster sheeting, they continued excavating the specimen, despite daily storms that tore away the tarps protecting the dinosaur's remains and threatened to flood the quarry.

While Currie hoped the specimen included a skull, experience had taught him how rare it is to find skulls with dinosaur skeletons. Two days of anticipation and disappointment resulted in success. Not much larger than the head of a rock hammer, the ornithomimid skull measures about 27 centimetres long and six centimetres high.

Finding the Skull

While Coy and the crew isolated the skeleton, Currie searched for the specimen's skull. Finding a dinosaur's skull is important — more than any other part of the body, it contains information about the animal's species, diet, age, evolutionary history and intelligence.

However, the odds against Currie finding a skull with this specimen were enormous. Skulls of ornithomimid dinosaurs are rare. The few that have been found are damaged — crushed and badly broken, with complete sections missing.

Starting where the jackhammer had shattered the dinosaur's neck, Currie set to work.

He isolated one vertebra, uncovering its edges. When he reached the end of it, no neighbouring neck bone could be found. He scraped around in the rock, but found nothing.

"It looks like this is it," he told the crew working around him. "We're not getting a skull."

Disappointed, he cleaned the bone he had found. He spent the next hour scraping away sandstone around the fossil. As he dug a little deeper, the rock crumbled and revealed more bone.

"Wait! There's some more here."

It was part of the next neck bone. Again, he isolated it, but could find no other bone leading from it.

"That really is the end," he announced.

Another hour passed as he cleaned the new vertebra. More sandstone crumbled away from his awl, and another bone came to light.

"Maybe not! There's another one!" Nine times, Currie and the crew swung between disappointment and hope. For two days, vertebra by vertebra, the neck slowly appeared. It was spiralling into the earth so that each bone rested deeper in the ground.

As Currie scraped deeper into the rock after the eighth vertebra, he again found more bone. But this wasn't vertebra. This was skull.

Holes pierced the rock all around — the jackhammer bit had missed the fragile fossil by only centimetres.

Bird-Mimic Chronicles:
Growing Up

As he and his family crossed their territory many times during the stormy, rainy months, the young Ornithomimus discovered the kinds of places where crawlers and winged buzzers lived — picking up the plump, tasty larvae with his claws and chasing older insects as they tried to escape his raking claws and beak. He hunted for lightning-quick lizards that darted through the undergrowth and up trees during the heat of the day — learning they weren't as quick early in the morning and on cool, wet days. He tried eating the spiky leaves of cone-bearing trees, but found the leaves he combed from the branches of gingko, sycamore and maple-like trees tastier. Wiry horsetails growing in wetlands caused stomach pains unless he ate tender, young growth; water lettuce was a plentiful substitute.

As days lengthened and storms became less frequent, trees and shrubs responded to the increasing hours of sunlight by putting forth new growth, and green shoots sprouted in the barren ground.

The ornithomimid family retraced its steps northward, heading for summer territories that would soon be lush with new vegetation. They encountered huge

herds of horned dinosaurs returning to coastal summer grounds. The duck-billed dinosaurs that had passed the winter alone or in small, family groups on the plain were also on the move, heading toward their breeding and nesting grounds.

Spring was coming.

Now almost two years old, the young dinosaur and his siblings developed adult features. Their bodies grew to fit their long legs, their muscles bulked up and they lost the scrawny proportions of juveniles. His one surviving sister retained the same dull colours she had hatched with, but he and his brothers became wonders — vivid russets, browns and scarlets striped the grey-brown of their hides from their heads to the tips of their tails, announcing to all other ornithomimids that they were young males of mating age.

But whenever he and his brothers showed off their colours, their father turned on them, hissing, pecking and swiping at them. Their father became more and more hostile as days passed — one brother was kicked in the ribs — forcing the young dinosaurs to keep their distance. Now, when the family travelled, the young males trailed behind, confused and uncertain, but still wanting desperately to be part of the family.

As they neared the breeding grounds, they met other groups of ornithomimids — each with young males following at a distance. The outcasts banded together. Unusual impulses were pushing at the young Ornitho-mimus, leaving him ever more bewildered. Whenever a female came near, or even looked in his direction, he found himself arching his neck and strutting so she could see how long his tail was, how strong his legs were, how handsome he looked ... In the evenings, he spent hours scraping nests in the ground ... and then sleeping beside them. If he was successful in hunting, instead of eating his catch he often found himself offering it to the nearest female; older males frequently intervened, making him retreat. Sometimes he dropped the food in his confusion — leaving it for the male to eat or to present to the female himself.

Around him, other young males were doing similar things. Sensing they were somehow competing with him, he tried asserting himself as their leader. He tested the fighting tactics his father had demonstrated so effectively to him and his brothers, but the other ornithomimids stood up to him, hissing and posturing back.

The squabbles were never serious — a couple of pecks and a slash of claws — and the combatants would retreat in alarm.

Modern Counterparts for an Ancient Animal

O ccasionally, traces of animal behaviour are preserved in the fossil record. Footprints, trackways, fossilized dung and bite marks in bone are suggestions of how animals lived.

However, to gain a clearer understanding of the possibilities of ancient behaviour, scientists look to modern animals. By studying animals alive today, palaeontologists interpret biology of ancient animals not preserved in the fossil record, including behaviour, soft-tissue structure, habitat and ecology.

Scientists believe basic behaviour reflects body shape. If so, then two different species that look the same should act in a similar fashion — making the ostrich a living **model** for *Ornithomimus*.

ostrich

Ostriches are members of a group of birds called the Ratites, which also include emus, cassowaries, kiwis and rheas. All are flightless, land-dwelling birds with stubby wings, egg-shaped bodies, powerful legs, small heads and long necks.

- The ostrich runs to avoid predators — its long, strong legs are proportioned for speed. The long, speed-proportioned leg bones of *Ornithomimus*, coupled with a lack of other obvious defences, suggest bird-mimic dinosaurs also ran to evade danger.

- As with most ornithomimids, ostriches are toothless, having replaced teeth with a beak.

- The huge eyes of *Ornithomimus* were about the same size as an ostrich's eyes. The parts of the skulls that encased the brains are about equally developed, indicating *Ornithomimus* had keen eyesight, good hearing and an adequate sense of smell, as ostriches do today.

Models only support or refute hypotheses; they don't prove theories. We will never be certain how *Ornithomimus* behaved, what colour it was, how quickly it grew or whether male ornithomimids

looked different than females. To understand non-fossilizing biology, we will always rely on hypotheses based on indirect evidence and modern models.

Controversy about ornithomimid behaviour is fuelled by an unusual combination of physical traits found within *Ornithomimus*. Today these same traits are found today only separately among very different groups of animals; their presence together in *Ornithomimus* presents a confusing picture of how the dinosaur lived.

Ornithomimid skulls indicate that the animals had some degree of overlapping vision, which would have allowed them to measure distances and hunt other animals for food. However, the eyes are placed on the sides of the dinosaur's narrow head, enabling good peripheral vision — a key trait of prey animals.

Enormous eyes may suggest that bird-mimic dinosaurs lived in open areas, using their eyes to spot approaching predators — as big-eyed ostriches do today. Huge eyes could also mean that *Ornithomimus* was most active at night.

Ornithomimus's beak was straight and blunt, lacking the hook seen on the beaks of modern hunter or scavenger birds. Crows, however, have straight, blunt beaks, and are known to hunt and to scavenge, as well as to eat seeds and fruit. Perhaps bird-mimic dinosaurs ate diets as varied as that of a crow.

Scientists estimate the claws of bird-mimic dinosaurs to have been about one-third the length of the entire hand, or about 10 to 15 centimetres long in adult ornithomimids. Such long, straight claws are similar to the claws of modern anteaters, suggesting that the dinosaurs dug for insects to eat.

However, bird-mimic's long, slender arms and narrow shoulders are not the powerful, sturdy, shovelling limbs of a digging animal.

Research by palaeontologist Elizabeth Nicholls, a Royal Tyrrell Museum of Palaeontology curator, on the shoulders, arms and hands of *Struthiomimus* indicates that this cousin to *Ornithomimus* probably used its hands more as hooks and clamps than for grasping, raking or digging. *Struthiomimus* may have fed on leaves and small twigs that it dragged to its mouth with its hands.

No similar studies have been done for *Ornithomimus*; the two species may have had very different diets and habits.

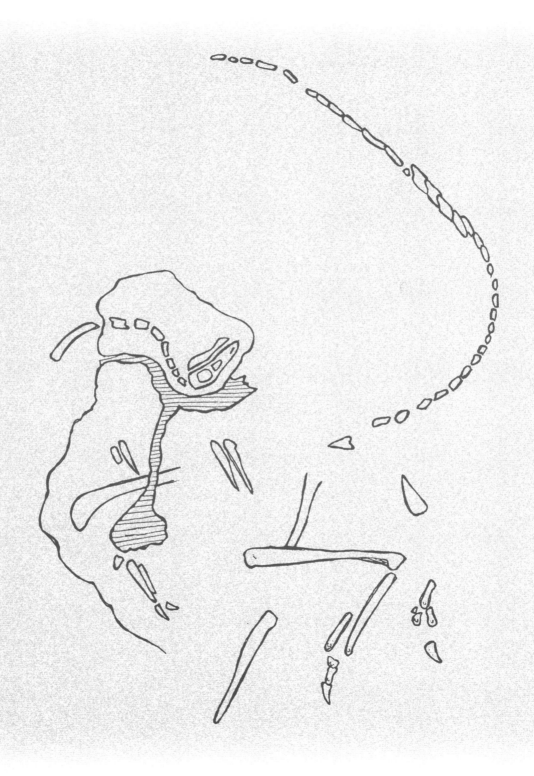

3. Fossil Research

Transport

When the position of the skeleton within the quarry had been determined, the crew began trenching around it. As they cut through the rock, they jacketed the fossils.

The animal's long tail curved away from the main body block. It was separated from the rest of the skeleton, decreasing the size of the largest fossil-and-rock block.

Just 13 days after it was discovered, the remains of the dinosaur were ready to be moved to the lab at the museum.

First, the crew carried the tail block down the hill on a stretcher.

Then, park staff, technicians and volunteers gathered at the quarry to help move the body block. Securing long cables around the 400-kilogram block, they dragged it across the quarry and lowered it down the hill. At the bottom of the hill, a backhoe lifted the block and carried it across the rugged valley bottom to the road, where a trailer awaited.

The 1.5-metre-long tail block was small enough to be carried out (top right), but the larger, heavier body block had to be lowered down the hill on a sled (top left). Heavy equipment eased its removal.

Food for Theropods

Palaeontologists theorizing about dinosaur behaviour can identify what most theropods ate: long, saw-edged, dagger-like teeth suggest diets of meat. Duck-billed- and horned-dinosaur bones with tooth marks and gashes matching

the shape and edges of theropod teeth indicate these plant eaters were food for hungry, meat-eating dinosaurs.

Diets of toothless, beaked theropods such as *Ornithomimus* are more mysterious. Scientists suggest plants, fruit,

insects, fish, eggs or small animals such as lizards and mammals. It could be bird-mimic dinosaurs ate anything edible they could find and fit into their mouths.

A recent discovery indicates that ornithomimids — as many birds do today — swallowed stones, which they stored in their stomachs to help grind food. The presence of these **gastroliths** suggests a diet of tough and fibrous plant material. However, no fossilized food has ever been found in an ornithomimid stomach; until that discovery is made, what they ate remains guesswork.

While nobody knows exactly what *Ornithomimus* ate, scientists believe bird-mimic dinosaurs were most often eaten by tyrannosaurs and dromaeosaurs — two groups of predatory dinosaurs common at the time.

The Fastest Dinosaur on Earth

Long foot bones put a real spring into *Ornithomimus's* step. As the dinosaur stepped down, energy from that movement was stored in the ligaments and tendons of the lower leg and ankle. This stored energy would then be released as thrust when the foot pushed off. Similar spring-like structures can be found in the feet of modern horses and in the backs of cheetahs.

Ornithomimus was built for speed. Estimates put top running speeds of the fast-moving dinosaurs at about 60 kilometres per hour — well above the speeds tyrannosaurs are thought to have reached.

The estimates are based on leg structure. Having long legs is important, but the difference between successful sprinters and those they leave behind is in the proportions of bones in the legs. As track-and-field athletes can appreciate, the longer the lower parts of the leg compared to the upper leg, the longer the stride. *Ornithomimus* was a step ahead of Olympic sprinters, with long foot bones.

The dinosaur also packed muscle into its upper legs to power its stride, and lightened its lower legs by reducing the number of toes. Construction of its hips allowed for rapid leg swing as *Ornithomimus* pumped its legs while running.

Bird-Mimic Chronicles:
Mating

At last the ornithomimids reached the nesting grounds. Many families had arrived earlier, so there was much pushing and trampling as males fought for and defended territories.

Forced from the safety near the centre of the group, the young Ornithomimus found himself scraping his attempts at a nest beneath a tall sycamore tree at the edge of the nesting grounds. His small territory included a number of trees among tall ferns and bushes. He trampled the shrubs surrounding the nest to create a clearing. Other young males wanted his space, but instinct made him fight hard to keep it.

Unfortunately, the females noticed neither his valour nor his housekeeping skills. They ignored all the males, moving to nearby streams and stands of trees where they could feed in peace. Males approached them continually, chests puffed out and heads bobbing, but the females merely wandered away. If a male was aggressive, the harassed female would hammer his chest and sides with quick, powerful kicks — sure to cool the interest of any suitor.

Uncertain of himself and not wanting to leave his hard-won nest open to competitors, the young Ornithomimus rarely ventured forth.

Early one morning, when leaves budded on the branches of his sycamore tree and blooms on nearby bushes spiced the air, he awoke from a nap to see, through the screen of fronds, a young female inspecting his nest. The sun dappled her back with light, her golden eyes were huge and round. The young Ornithomimus raised his head to look at her over the ferns; she started, surprised by his presence and ready to bound away, but he made no move. They simply stared at each other.

She relaxed and returned to inspecting the nest, keeping him within sight. He slowly rose and stepped through the ferns. She tensed again, watching from the corner of her eye. He lowered his head at her, displaying his colours. When she didn't move away, he straightened and regarded her further. Uncertain, he puffed out his chest and raked the ground with his long claws. She turned, and stretched her neck toward him. Her attention encouraged him; he tentatively huffed at her, his lungs forcing air out through his snout, and bobbed his head. She started to bob back when she caught herself and stopped, surprised at her reaction.

He bobbed again, and this time she allowed herself to reply. He slowly lifted one foot high off the ground, balancing carefully, and suddenly slammed it down hard, causing dirt to fly.

He stamped again and again. Gradually the pace increased, feet thudding, sand flying, head bobbing, tail whipping and lungs booming. Suddenly, he stopped and stood still, staring at her. She arched her neck, huffed and stamped once …

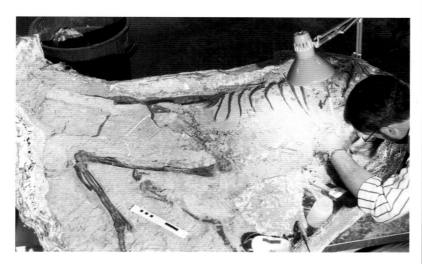

To stabilize the fragile fossils, Coy soaks them with preservative glue, strengthening them and cementing them to the supporting rock.

Preparation

As soon as the specimen was installed in the lab at the Royal Tyrrell Museum, Coy started removing the rock that encased the bones.

He found the sandstone **matrix** soft and easy to separate from the fossils. Beneath, the *Ornithomimus*'s bones were well preserved, but brittle. When one broke, as cannot always be avoided, its insides disintegrated into dust, leaving only the hard, shiny, outer shell.

Not all preparation went according to plan. The last few

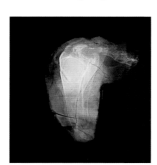

neck vertebrae attached to the skull were so tightly fitted, there was no way to pry them apart and not damage — or destroy — the skull.

It was also too risky to mould the skull. Instead, Currie scanned the skull at medical laboratories in Calgary, Alberta, and Salem, Oregon. The results show, in places, bone thinner than a sheet of paper.

Bones less than one-tenth of a millimetre thick at the front of the skull contribute to the rarity of finding complete, intact ornithomimid skulls.

The Inside Scoop

Currie used digital scanning technology to look at the shape of spaces and bones inside the *Ornithomimus* skull.

Computed tomography uses x-rays to measure the density of an object in cross-section. Information from the scans is fed into a computer where software organizes it to create three-dimensional images, to reveal internal structures or shapes of cavities or to visually enhance parts or structures of the object.

Normally used by doctors to find and identify medical problems inside a person's body, the technology works well with fossils when the density between bone and matrix differ. Computed tomography has helped palaeontologists around the world better understand the ancient animals they study by mapping the interiors of rare specimens.

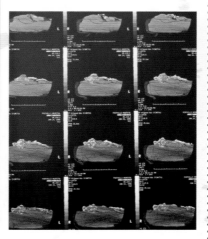

Only by examining hundreds of cross-section scans of the specimen can Currie make sense of the bone structure and arrangement of the ornithomimid skull.

Palaeontology draws upon many sciences and disciplines to make sense of animals and environments that have long since disappeared (right).

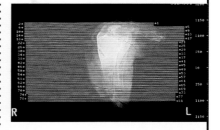

The bar code-like picture of the skull shows where the scans cross-sectioned the fossil.

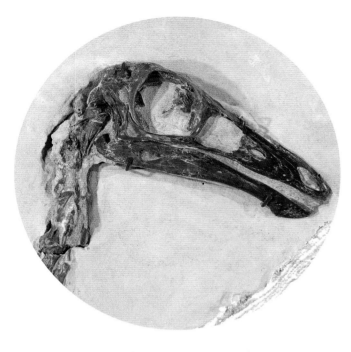

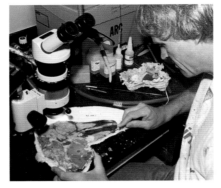

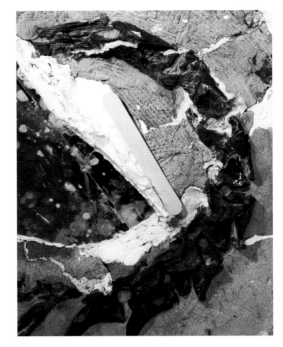

Preservation

As the skull was prepared, its scientific value became clear. Although slightly squished from side to side, its profile and **sutures** — the place where two separate bones meet — are so well preserved that Currie was able to map how the bones fit together. In all ornithomimid skulls found previously, the front bones are crushed, leaving cracks and fractures that are difficult to distinguish from sutures.

The sutures on this specimen tell Currie the shape and size of the head, and also the age of the dinosaur when it died. In very young animals — including humans — skull bones are separate from one another, held in place by soft tissues. As animals age, the edges of these bones slowly grow into each other and new bone knits them together. In older animals, the sutures disappear completely.

In the *Ornithomimus* specimen, the sutures are clearly visible, but none of the bones are free from each other — suggesting that the animal had recently reached full growth when it died 76 million years ago.

The specimen's skeleton is equally well preserved. It is 98 percent complete, with only bones from the leg, arm and hand missing. The animal's entire shoulder area is articulated, even with bones broken by the jackhammer. Coy recorded the positions of the shoulder bones and prepared them completely so **moulds** could be made for research.

He then pieced together the jackhammered bones. Amazingly, the breaks were clean enough that everything fitted together.

More than any other part of a dinosaur's skeleton, its skull provides scientists with information about the animal's species, diet, age, relationships to other dinosaurs and relative intelligence (top centre).

Coy likens rebuilding the shattered fossil bones to reconstructing a fine china vase (bottom centre and above).

"Because the insides had crumbled away, I had to build up these thin walls of bone around hollow, empty space. There were literally hundreds of tiny bits and slivers to fit together."

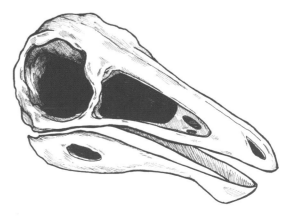

Bird-Mimic Chronicles:
Nesting

The *Ornithomimus* was content. Guarding the 18 eggs in his nest, he dozed in the late-afternoon sun. The daily rain shower had cleared the early-summer haze from the air, and water drops ran off the broad green leaves of the sycamore overhead, gently sprinkling him and the sandy ground.

The female was away feeding. From a distance, he could hear her and others of his kind moving through the brush. Birds fluttered in the trees around him, silent but for their wing beats. It was their nesting season, too.

Standing, the Ornithomimus stretched. He walked to the edge of the clearing and peered through the bushes, scanning for predators and egg eaters.

The sound of flapping wings spun him around. A **pterosaur** [TAIR-oh-sor] landed in the nest, its mate fluttering in the branches above. Using its beak, it hammered open the shell of an egg.

The Ornithomimus lunged. Flying reptiles had already destroyed several of the eggs. Snapping with his beak, he tore a piece of skin from the creature's wing as it leapt away, veering out of reach. The ornithomimid gave chase, springing across the clearing and huffing great, angry booms.

Behind him, the other pterosaur darted down and jabbed its beak into another egg, cracking the shell open and spilling its contents. As the Ornithomimus spun around, the pterosaur grabbed the unborn dinosaur and leapt into the air, flapping to the upper branches of the sycamore. There, it and its mate fought over their prize while the dinosaur stamped and huffed below.

After they finished eating, they teased the ornithomimid, trying to approach the nest again, but the dinosaur had learned their tricks; he stood guard over the eggs. Help arrived as his mate bounded through the trees, calling to him. She had seen the flying reptiles and heard his calls.

At her approach, the pterosaurs flew off.

The Ornithomimus stepped carefully inside the ring of eggs and crouched protectively over them.

Six days later, in the warmth and shelter of his body, 16 beautiful baby ornithomimids hatched, naked bodies mottled blue and red and huge eyes bulging from wobbly, oversized heads.

. . .

Hollow Bones

Whenever *Ornithomimus* ran, it subjected its bones to enormous stresses. The act of pushing off the ground with one foot and landing with the other would have bent, twisted, pulled and pressed at the animal's leg and foot bones. *Ornithomimus* would have needed a strong skeleton to withstand such stresses. It also would have needed light bones to be able to move as quickly and efficiently as scientists believe it did.

Nature's solution to the problem faced by *Ornithomimus* and other theropod dinosaurs was the hollow **cylinder**. Hollow bones are strong, lightweight and capable of resisting enormous, complicated stresses. Engineers have found that when they try to bend, twist or pull a cylinder, stress is greatest at the object's surface and least at its centre. With the surface absorbing most of the stress, the interior is not needed. By hollowing the cylinder, strength and resistance is maintained, and weight is reduced.

Scientists have found the material that makes up the thin walls of theropod bones to be much denser than the porous bone of plant-eating dinosaurs. This density, concentrated in the walls of *Ornithomimus*'s hollow bones, would have provided increased strength exactly where the animal needed it most.

The ornithomimids' long leg bones are further strengthened by a slight increase in diameter and wall thickness mid-length, where the length is otherwise most likely to bend.

Having thin-walled, hollow bones helped theropods save energy. Not only did the dinosaurs work less to move their light bones around, but also less energy was required to build and maintain them. The animals would have used the energy savings for other purposes important for survival, such as hunting down the next meal or caring for young.

It was a short evolutionary step to fill the centres of hollow bones with air sacs, as are seen in birds today. Air sacs would have further lightened the bones and decreased the amount of energy the animals needed to move around.

Today, bicycle makers capitalize on this phenomenon to make ever stronger and lighter bicycle frames.

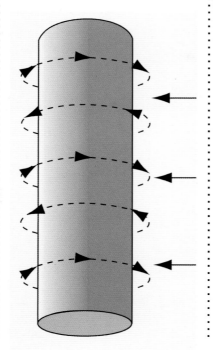

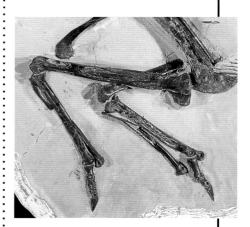

The oval shape of the bones' cylindrical cross-section adds strength.

The tonnes of accumulated sediment pressing down on the fossilizing skeleton collapsed the *Ornithomimus*'s long, hollow leg bones.

Evolution of Beaks and Tooth- lessness

Ornithomimids were small, lightly built animals with long necks. Reducing the weight of the skull and neck would have provided energy-saving advantages over heavier relatives, and would have increased the animal's speed and agility.

Ornithomimids did this by evolving ever thinner, more hollow bones, and by replacing teeth with lighter beaks. The most primitive bird-mimic specimens retain teeth, demonstrating steps in the evolution of toothlessness among this group of theropods: *Pelecanimimus* from Spain has hundreds of tiny teeth in both jaws; *Harpymimus* from Asia has teeth only in the front, lower jaw. Toothlessness in ornithomimids may have come about as they reduced the size of each tooth while increasing the number of teeth. Some scientists believe the teeth became so tiny, just one small evolutionary step further stopped a few teeth from growing at all, and another tiny step stopped a few more ... leading eventually to elimination of all teeth.

The replacement — a beak — is an evolutionary solution to toothlessness that is found in birds, turtles and some whales, as well as in ornithomimids. Made of keratin, the same tough protein fingernails are made of, beaks grow constantly. Over generations, their shape can be adapted to do almost anything — from cracking nuts, tearing flesh or gathering insects to filter feeding, building nests or storing food.

cracking tearing storing gathering beak

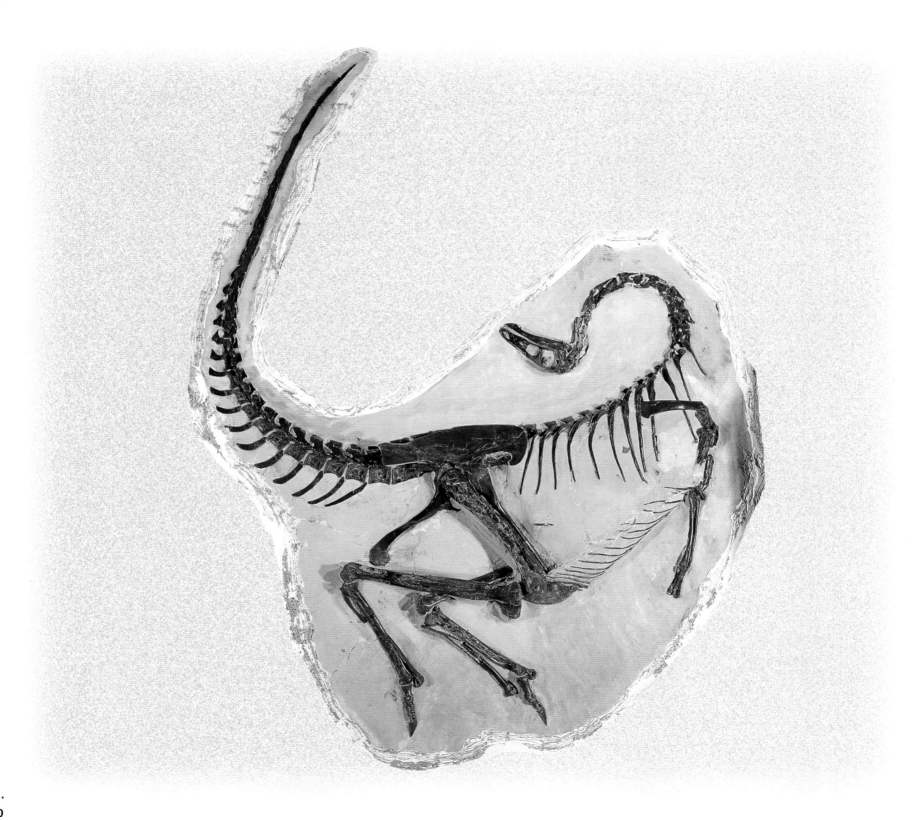

4. A Second Life

Ornithomimus Discoveries

The *Ornithomimus* specimen discovered in 1995 is the first-known, non-flying dinosaur fossil with part of a beak still attached to its jaws.

In ornithomimid fossils found previously, the outer edges of the jaws are riddled with tiny fossilized blood vessels. These blood vessels must have been feeding a part of the body not preserved with the bones. As ornithomimids were toothless, scientists speculated

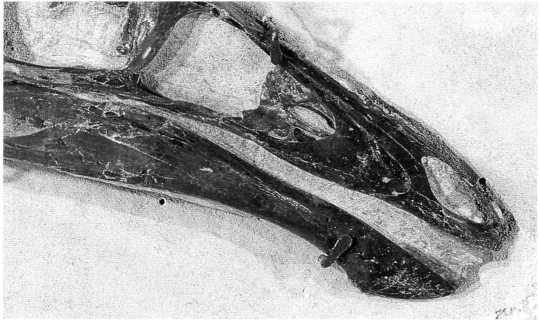

that the missing, non-fossilizing part of the body was a beak — the dinosaurs must have evolved something to replace teeth.

Beaks are not an unusual solution to toothlessness — birds, turtles and some whales have beaks. It seemed likely that ornithomimids were also beaked.

The 1995 specimen moves the idea that bird-mimic dinosaurs had beaks out of the realm of speculation and into the realm of indisputable fact.

"This specimen tells us the beak on *Ornithomimus edmontonensis* was probably sharp and cutting," says Currie. "Its jaw bones fit together tightly, with little overlap; a beak would have provided an effective cutting edge — good for nipping the heads off of little animals, or fronds off of ferns."

X-rays reveal the size and shape of the part of the specimen's skull that had encased the brain.

"These animals probably had a good sense of sight," says Currie, "which we suspected because of the size of their eyes. The bones around the ear region suggest they were able to hear both high- and low-frequency sounds — so they probably had keen hearing, too. The **olfactory** region of the brain is well developed, but the scans show fairly small nasal chambers, so maybe ornithomimids didn't have as good a sense of smell as we like to think they did."

In fact, while the ornithomimid **braincase** is slightly smaller than that of an ostrich, the areas developed within the braincase are similar to those of the bird-mimic dinosaur's

modern counterpart. A brain of that size and complexity would have been a remarkable evolutionary advantage for a dinosaur.

Black marks speckling the surface of one of the specimen's arm bones puzzle palaeontologists.

"We had some very fine-tuned analyses done using Atomic Energy Canada's facilities in Chalk River, Ontario, to find out what these marks are," says Currie. "But the quantities of minerals causing the colour are so minute, we couldn't isolate them from surrounding rock. All we can say is the markings are a mineral compound perceived visually, but not chemically."

There is speculation that the markings represent preservation of feathers. As more feathered dinosaurs come to

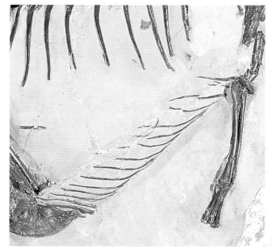

light in China every year, the possibility that ornithomimids also had some kind of feathering becomes better worth considering. However, until a bird-mimic specimen is found with clear feather impressions, feathers on ornithomimids remain speculation.

The presence and position of stomach ribs in the specimen changed views on the shape of bird-mimic dinosaurs. Before this specimen was found, some scientists thought ornithomimids were slighter animals, but these ribs — or **gastralia** — show they had deep chests.

Gastralia suggest ornithomimids, just as birds do today, used abdominal air sacs as well as their lungs to breathe. The cage of bones enclosing the abdomen would have helped pump air into and out of these air sacs — just as diaphragm muscles in the belly of mammals force air into and out of lungs.

This kind of pumping would have increased the dinosaurs' oxygen-processing efficiency by about 25 percent, helping them to reach the 60-kilometre-per-hour speeds of which scientists believe ornithomimids were capable.

Ornithomimids had unusual wrists for theropod dinosaurs. In birds and many theropods of the same time, wrist bones are fused, creating pulley-like joints that allowed for quick, grabbing movements and for folding the arms. In ornithomimids, they are not fused and they contain more bones. Researchers think early bird-mimic dinosaurs did have fused joints, but their descendants lost them over time as they developed their own arrangement of wrist bones.

The separation and arrangement of bones in ornithomimid wrists would have made for a greater range of movement than birds have. It also suggests a close relationship with tyrannosaurs, which have similar wrists.

Evolution of Feathers and Flight

Scientists have debated how birds took to the air since the discovery of *Archaeopteryx* in 1862. This **Jurassic**-bird skeleton has claws on two fingers, no chest keel and a very small **sternum**. Based on this evidence, some scientists propose that powered, flapping flight developed from gliding — early birds climbed trees using their claws and, as flying squirrels do today, jumped and spread their arms to glide from tree to tree.

Other scientists believe flapping flight evolved when theropod dinosaurs used their arms for balance and quick direction changes while chasing prey.

The wrists of dinosaurs such as *Dromaeosaurus* are pulley-like joints that would have enabled the dinosaurs to snap their arms forward to grasp prey. This quick, snatching movement resembles the flight stroke of modern birds. The dinosaurs that gave rise to birds likely used this adaptation while running — as predators, they had to chase prey. Running birds today use their wings to maintain balance and turn sharply, and young birds often flap their wings while running to gain speed. The small amounts of lift generated by the flapping arms of running theropod dinosaurs may have been the first steps toward powered flight.

Feathers also increase lift. However, just as scientists think the flight stroke developed from movements originally used for another purpose, they also believe flight feathers developed from feathers that had other functions.

Tiny theropod dinosaurs found in northeastern China in the 1990s show evidence of feathers. On *Sinosauropteryx*, the feathers seem to be a downy covering that provided insulation. Other specimens — including *Caudipteryx* and *Protarchaeopteryx* — show feathers that may have helped attract mates. Fossils of **Confuciusornis** [kon-FOO-shus-ORN-us], a bird with tail and wing feathers that would have enabled it to fly, are found in the same rocks.

Feathers are adaptations of scales. Laboratory experiments have proven that, by changing the way a bird's body makes proteins, scientists can cause feathers to develop from the scales on the bird's feet.

It is believed that feathers evolved from dinosaur scales before the appearance of tyrannosaurs and bird-mimic dinosaurs, making it possible that *Tyrannosaurus* and *Ornithomimus* had their own coverings of feathers.

Top photo: O. Louis Mazzatenta

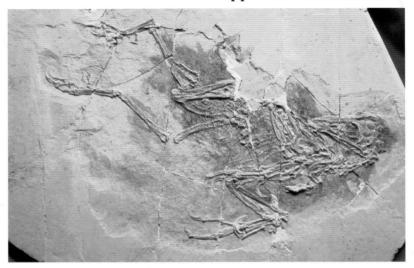

The dark, smudged halo radiating from the neck and back of this juvenile Sinosauropteryx skeleton (top) may be the fossilized remains of downy feathers. Unlike many of the feathered dinosaurs of the same period and region, Confuciusornis (above) had feathers that would have permitted flight. Many palaeontologists believe flight is what distinguishes birds from feathered dinosaurs — even though some groups of birds have since lost the ability to fly.

If *Ornithomimus* had feathers, they likely would have helped the animal maintain body temperature and possibly compete for mates and breeding territory. In addition to making flight possible, feathers serve similar functions in modern birds.

Bird-Mimic Chronicles:
Flight and Fall

Summer was not kind to the young dinosaur family. Many youngsters were lost despite the parents' watchfulness — some to **troodontids** and giant lizards that lurked around the edges of the ornithomimid nesting grounds; some to pterosaurs. Sometimes other ornithomimids took advantage of the parents' inexperience and lapses in attention to snatch easy meals.

By the time the nestlings were ready to leave the trampled nesting plain for richer, less-harvested hunting grounds, only six were left.

Other families that had nested nearby had been departing, one by one, for weeks as days shortened and trees and shrubs changed colour. The Ornithomimus and his family started their journey the day great gusts of wind blew the yellow leaves from the sycamore that had sheltered their home.

They moved slowly across the plain, pausing frequently to feed and find shelter from the worst of the rainy weather.

Other animals were also on the move. Flocks of birds flew south. Families of heavily armoured dinosaurs trudged across the land, browsing the high ground as they went. Horned dinosaurs moved to their winter territories.

One stormy day, the family paused in its travels to watch a group of duck-billed dinosaurs cross a river. Pounding rain had fallen for days; in the roaring flood, the younger, smaller duckbills were swept away, bawling for their mothers as they struggled across the current. A pack of dromaeosaurs, attracted by the cries, had caught a youngster staggering weakly ashore downstream and were feeding on it.

The Ornithomimus's mate led their children away. But he stayed back, curious about the fate of the duckbills — he and his family also had to find a way across the flood.

Hammering rain, rushing water and the distressed trumpeting of the duck-bills filled his ears. He didn't hear the stick breaking in the trees behind him. He didn't see the trembling bushes.

It was instinct that turned his head in time to see four young albertosaurs charging toward him.

Instant, total panic dropped over him. He turned and ran — ran blindly; ran desperately; ran as he had never run before; ran knowing he was going to die. Albertosaurs weren't supposed to get so close he could hear them breathing. And these were young — faster and more agile than adults and meaner than the sickle-claws that were feeding on the baby duckbill behind him. And there were four of them … no, five — another Albertosaurus burst from the trees, dashing to cut him off …

The Ornithomimus raced on, thighs pumping, feet pushing, heart slamming, neck stretched forward as he reached desperately for safety …

He wasn't going to make it. They were going to cut him off, chase him down, tear him open … He ran, barely aware of the river raging on one side, filling its steep, sharp banks and cutting away at its edges. A rumble and crash boomed as a tall pine tottered on the bank and fell, tearing the ground almost beneath the Ornithomimus's feet.

Then he saw it. Ahead, right where the albertosaurs were driving him, was a bend in the racing river. They were going to trap him against the water!

Despair creeping into his panic, his eyes searched for an escape. There was none — only the river.

The Ornithomimus made his choice. Digging deep into his last reserves of strength, he charged to the river, picking up speed and measuring the distance to the bank.

With one giant leap he threw himself off the edge and into the air, the huge jaws of an Albertosaurus snapping at his tail. Time seemed to slow as he pedalled headlong over the churning tree trunks, reaching for the shore that was so far away. He had the sensation of drifting in a quiet bubble over a world of noise and terror as the bank ever so slowly neared.

As suddenly as the drifting feeling had arrived, it fled. Water and bank rushed up at him, and he slammed into the ground, tumbling over and over in the wet dirt.

He had made it.

At the very edge of the water, his claws had cut deep into the soggy soil.

A quick glimpse back through the curtains of driving rain showed the albertosaurs on the far bank, roaring and stamping in frustration.

The Ornithomimus staggered upright and reeled away from the river.

Cause of Death

During preparation, Coy discovered three broken bones that could not have been fractured by the jackhammer. Located in the upper arm and shoulder, the breaks are jagged and very old. The splintered ends of one arm bone ride up over one another.

Coy asked the coroner at the Drumheller Hospital to examine the specimen. The doctor was unable to prove the breaks had happened before the ornithomimid's death. However, he stated that similar injuries in a human could cause death from **shock**.

Currie believes they occurred shortly before the animal died and may have caused the *Ornithomimus*'s death.

"If these bones were broken after death — either by being crushed or simply from a lot of sediment piling up on top of them or something standing on them — the ribs underneath them would be crushed. They aren't, and they are much more delicate than these bones."

No one will ever know how the *Ornithomimus* was injured or if the bones broke soon after death.

However, the breaks are similar to the injuries a two-legged animal would receive if it tripped and fell while running. When such accidents happen today to high-speed creatures such as cheetahs and ostriches, they are often deadly — either killing the animal outright or causing such **trauma** it dies soon afterward.

Although we will never know for sure why the *Ornithomimus* died, the breaks in its arm and shoulder are possible causes.

Bird-Mimic Chronicles:
Death and Cover-up

As he stumbled away from the water's edge, the Ornithomimus realized he was in trouble. He was very, very tired and very, very sore. He could neither lift nor move his arm — the pain in his shoulder wracked his body with spasms.

And he was cold. He couldn't stop shivering. Driving rain, blasting wind and creeping dampness seemed to seep through his hide into his bones.

On the shore of a weed-choked pond near the river, he found shelter among the ferns and bare bushes. He collapsed beneath a spreading sycamore tree.

He lost consciousness. His injury was so severe, the breaks in his shoulder and arm so grave, his blood pressure plummeted and he sank into a coma.

As he lay, rain continued to pour down. The river filled its course, swirling with mud and debris. Working at the bank, it found a weak spot in the sand and dirt. It burst through, loosing its load of sand and silt over the ground. It quickly found the pond and poured its sediment into the stagnant water, forming a swirling, muddy pool that crept toward the sycamore tree and the unconscious body nestled beneath.

As the flood rose around the tree's roots and then its trunk, the water lifted the Ornithomimus and whirled him gently around the pool before cutting a way out of the basin and flowing on.

At first, the dinosaur floated, turning over so his injured arm and his head dragged through the drowned shrubs and waving water weeds.

His barely breathing lungs filled with water. The dinosaur died peacefully as he sank onto a watery bed of weeds and fallen leaves.

There his body lay for days as water flowed over him. The flesh holding his limbs together slowly decayed, and a few bones washed a short distance away.

Even after the rain stopped, it took weeks for the water to recede. The river had forced a new path for itself through sandbars, gravel banks and mud and silt. It now curved through the pond, following an older, long-abandoned oxbow channel before cutting across the plain toward the distant sea. As the current slowed and river levels dropped, the sediment carried in by the river settled over the decaying leaves lying in the mud at the bottom, burying the dinosaur's body and filling the basin's bottom with fine, white sand.

Near the dinosaur's grave, behind a low sandbank deposited by the flood, the sycamore tree stood guard, the last of the season's golden leaves clinging to its branches.

Preparing the specimen for display was an involved process. Not only did the parts of the skeleton that had been separated have to be reassembled, but also the field jackets had to be adjusted (right). A steel frame, designed especially for the exhibit, cradles and supports the specimen (below).

Display

As preparation of the *Ornithomimus* neared completion, the bones were reassembled. The shoulder shattered by the jackhammer was put back together. The neck and skull were aligned with the rest of the body.

It was decided that **casts** from other specimens would not replace the missing hand and foot bones. And, because the side of the specimen that is displayed is the underside of the skeleton as it lay in the field, Coy did not need to reposition the leg bone that had been found metres away from the rest of the skeleton.

By keeping the field jacket around the specimen, the display would help visitors to the museum understand how fossils are collected and prepared for research. The specimen had been brought to the museum in four separate field jackets. Where each touched, the sides were removed, and burlap and plaster were used to create the illusion of a single jacket cradling the entire dinosaur. Where plaster had been poured to fill gaps and holes, matrix was glued to resemble the original sandstone.

The jacket and specimen were set within a steel frame to support the display.

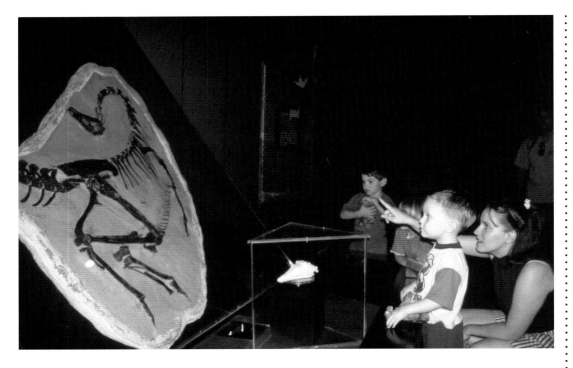

In the Gallery

In May 1997, less than two years after its discovery, the *Ornithomimus* was wheeled into the gallery of the Royal Tyrrell Museum of Palaeontology.

The *Ornithomimus* provided information that has helped scientists solve many longstanding mysteries about this puzzling group of dinosaurs. It has also prompted palaeontologists to ask many new questions. How did these dinosaurs live and interact with their environment? When and where did they first evolve? When did they develop beaks? For what purpose did they develop those unusually long claws? These questions will be answered only if — when — many more such specimens are discovered and studied.

The Search for Plant Fossils Continues

Palaeontologist Dennis Braman examines the fossils littering the slope before him. He is looking for plant fossils in Dinosaur Provincial Park, but all he sees today are champsosaur vertebrae, fish scales, shark teeth and broken bits of fossil bone. He notes the location in his field journal and moves on, continuing his quest for a site that contains leaves, twigs and branches of plants from an earlier time in the park's history.

Sites containing plant fossils such as petrified wood or coalified evergreen twigs have been located in Dinosaur Provincial Park. None, however, contain anything similar to the quality of flowering-plant fossils that were found in the *Ornithomimus* quarry.

Glossary

Albertosaurus [al-BERT-oh-SOR-us]: Large, meat-eating dinosaur that lived from 78 million to 68 million years ago. *Albertosaurus* was an early, smaller cousin to *Tyrannosaurus rex*.

Ankylosaur [an-KIGH-loh-sor]: Squat, four-legged, plant-eating dinosaur covered with bony plates and spikes.

Archaeopteryx [AR-kee-OP-ter-iks]: First-known fossilized bird. Found in Jurassic-aged rock in Germany.

Articulated: United by means of a joint. An articulated skeleton is one in which the bones are in place in relation to one another, as when the animal was alive.

Bird: Warm-blooded, feathered, egg-laying, two-legged vertebrate that can fly or is descended from animals that could fly. The ability to fly distinguishes birds from dinosaurs that had feathers.

Braincase: The part of a skull that contains the brain.

Cast: Three-dimensional form made from a mould.

Caudipteryx [KAW-dee-TAIR-iks]: Feathered dinosaur from northeastern China.

Compsognathus [COMP-sog-NAY-thus]: Small, meat-eating dinosaur that lived during the Jurassic period. Fossils are found in the same rock in Germany in which *Archaeopteryx* fossils are found.

Confuciusornis [kon-FOO-shus-ORN-us]: Early bird with display feathers on the tail. Fossils are found in northeastern China.

Cretaceous [kre-TAY-shus]: Geologic period dating from 140 million to 65 million years ago.

Cylinder: Long, circular body of uniform diametre.

Deinonychus [digh-NO-ni-kus]: First-known dromaeosaur species. The discovery of *Deinonychus* in the 1960s prompted scientists to speculate that some dinosaurs were warm-blooded and were ancestors of birds.

Dromaeosaur [DROH-mee-oh-sor]: Small, meat-eating dinosaur characterized by a large, crescent-shaped claw on the second toe of each hind foot. Alberta's **Dromaeosaurus** [DROH-mee-oh-SOR-us] is one kind of dromaeosaur.

Dromiceiomimus [DROH-mee-see-oh-MIGH-mus]: Bird-mimic dinosaur closely related to *Ornithomimus*. Fossils are found in North America.

Erosion: Process of gradual wearing away.

Field jacket: Protective covering made of layers of plaster and burlap applied to fossils to prevent damage due to exposure, transportation or preparation.

Fossil: Remains or a trace of ancient life at least 10,000 years old.

Fuse: To become one.

Gastralia [gas-TRAY-lee-uh]: Rib-like bones that cover the belly region of some animals.

Gastrolith [GAS-troh-lith]: Small stones eaten by some animal species and stored within their guts to help grind food.

Harpymimus [HAR-pee-MIGH-mus]: Early bird-mimic dinosaur with teeth. Fossils are found in Asia.

Jurassic [jer-AS-ik]: The middle geologic period of the Age of Dinosaurs. The Jurassic dates from about 205 million to 142 million years ago.

Mammal: Warm-blooded, fur-bearing animal that gives birth to live young and feeds its young milk that is produced within the mother's body. Humans are mammals.

Matrix: Rock in which a fossil is embedded.

Model: Object, animal or system studied by scientists to learn about other, similar things that cannot be studied firsthand.

Mould: Hollow, three-dimensional pattern used to create shapes.

Olfactory: Pertaining to the sense of smell.

Organic: Having to do with living things; made up of carbon compounds such as those found in living things.

Ornithomimid [Or-NITH-oh-MIGH-mid]: Small to medium-sized theropod dinosaur with a long tail, long neck, long legs, long arms and a beak. **Ornithomimus** [Or-NITH-oh-MIGH-mus] *edmontonensis* ("Bird-mimic from

Edmonton") is a species that belongs to the ornithomimid dinosaur group.

Oviraptor [OH-vee-RAP-ter]: Beaked, crested theropod dinosaur whose fossils are found in Asia.

Overburden: Rock above a specimen that must be removed in order to expose and collect a fossil.

Palaeontology: Study of ancient life through fossils. A **palaeontologist** is a scientist who studies ancient life through fossils.

Palynology: Study of fossil pollens, spores and cells. A **palynologist** is a scientist who studies ancient life through fossil pollens, spores and cells.

Pelecanimimus [PEH-leh-KAN-i-MIGH-mus]: Early bird-mimic dinosaur with teeth. Fossils are found in Spain.

Permineralization: Fossilization process by which groundwater minerals fill porous spaces within bone and wood.

Pollen: Powder-like male reproductive cells of flowering plants.

Predator: Animal that hunts other animals for food.

Prey: Animal that other animals hunt for food.

Protarchaeopteryx [proh-TAR-kee-OP-ter-iks]: Small, feathered, theropod dinosaur fossils found in northeastern China.

Pterosaur [TAIR-oh-sor]: Flying reptile that lived during the time of the dinosaurs. Pterosaurs were not dinosaurs.

Quarry: Place where rocks containing fossils are excavated.

Replacement: Fossilization process by which organic minerals within bone are replaced by inorganic minerals. It can also include the entire replacement of the original bone, wood, animal or plant with inorganic minerals.

Scavenger: Animal that eats animals that are already dead.

Sediment: Dirt, sand, dust and other particles deposited by wind or water.

Shock: Medical condition in which blood pressure drops, heart rate increases, circulation slows and, in extreme cases, the brain suffocates. Can be fatal if not treated promptly.

Sinornithosaurus [SIGN-or-NITH-oh-SOR-us]: First-known feathered dromaeosaur. Fossils are found in northeastern China.

Sinosauropteryx [SIGN-oh-sor-OP-ter-iks]: First-known feathered dinosaur. Fossilized feather impressions show a down-like covering. Found in northeastern China.

Species: Similar plants or animals that can mate and produce offspring that can also reproduce.

Specimen: Item that is representative of a larger group.

Spore: Reproductive body produced by ferns, mosses, algae, fungi, and so on, that is capable of giving rise to a new individual.

Sternum: The bony line down the chest where the two halves of the rib cage come together.

Struthiomimus [STRU-thee-oh-MIGH-mus]: North American, bird-mimic dinosaur.

Suture: Where two separate bones come together, or where two sides of a cut are brought together.

Theropod [THAIR-oh-pod]: Meat-eating dinosaur, or of the lineage of meat-eating dinosaurs.

Trauma: Severe injury.

Trench: Ditch, or to dig a ditch.

Triassic [tri-AS-ik]: The earliest geologic period of the Age of Dinosaurs, during which dinosaurs first appeared. The Triassic dates from about 250 million to 205 million years ago.

Troodon [TROH-oh-don]: Small, meat-eating dinosaur — believed to have been among the smartest of dinosaurs. **Troodontids** [TROH-oh-don-TIDS] are dinosaurs that belong to the *Troodon* group of dinosaurs.

Tyrannosaurus [tigh-RAN-oh-SOR-us]: Large meat-eating dinosaur, characterized by two fingers on each of its hands. *Tyrannosaurus* and *Albertosaurus* are both **tyrannosaurs** [tigh-RAN-oh-sors].

Vertebra: Back bone. A vertebrate is an animal with a backbone.

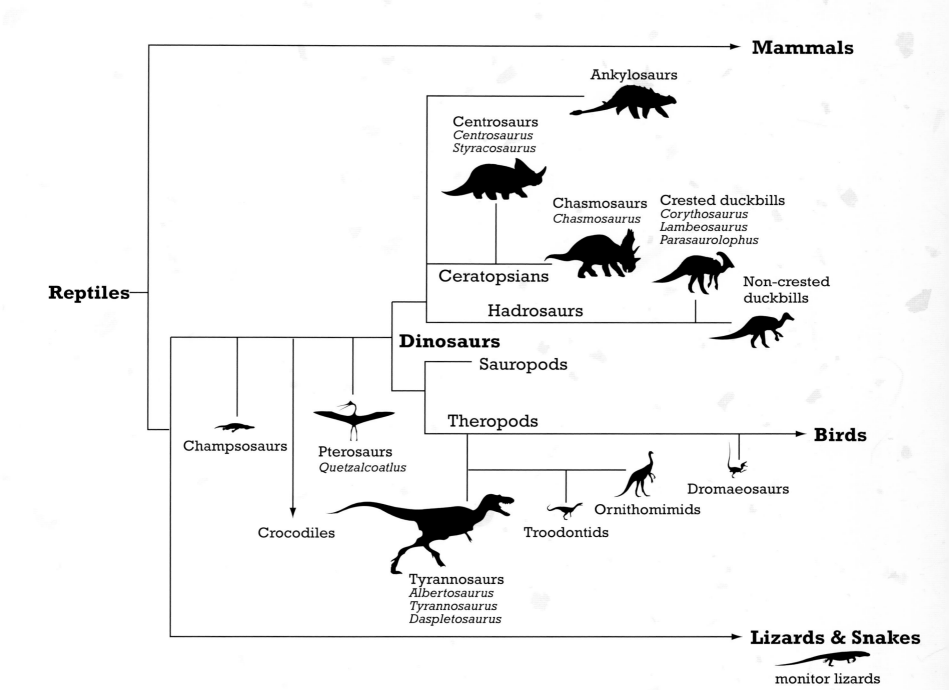

Mammals

Ankylosaurs

Centrosaurs
Centrosaurus
Styracosaurus

Chasmosaurs
Chasmosaurus

Crested duckbills
Corythosaurus
Lambeosaurus
Parasaurolophus

Ceratopsians

Non-crested
duckbills

Reptiles

Hadrosaurs

Dinosaurs

Sauropods

Theropods

Birds

Champsosaurs

Pterosaurs
Quetzalcoatlus

Dromaeosaurs

Ornithomimids

Crocodiles

Troodontids

Tyrannosaurs
Albertosaurus
Tyrannosaurus
Daspletosaurus

Lizards & Snakes

monitor lizards

Meet the Scientists

By studying fossil pollens and spores, palynologist **Dennis Braman** tries to solve ancient ecological mysteries, including what Late Cretaceous Alberta was like and what caused the disappearance of dinosaurs and other species 65 million years ago. His research indicates that long before a giant meteorite struck at the end of the Age of Dinosaurs, the extinction of plants, dinosaurs and many other species was already underway.

Dinosaur palaeontologist **Philip Currie** had long believed fossils of dinosaurs with feathers would be found somewhere, some day — it was just a matter of time. In 1996, when he was shown the first-known specimen of Chinese *Sinosauropteryx* with its halo of feather-like filaments, he was elated. Since then, he has examined many feathered-dinosaur specimens from northern China.

He also is researching evidence of social behaviour among large theropods at bonebeds in Alberta and Argentina.

Until he left to set up the fossil-preparation program at a Japanese museum in 1997, **Clive Coy** supervised Dinosaur Preparation at the Royal Tyrrell Museum. As well as helping excavate the *Ornithomimus*, he was its chief preparator. "I had the real sense of being the first person to see that magnificent specimen as it unfolded," he says. "Every area of it was a challenge."

Coy travelled to Ottawa and Toronto to study previously known bird-mimic dinosaur specimens to better understand the *Ornithomimus* specimen discovered in 1995.

Technician **Kevin Aulenback** has been with the Royal Tyrrell Museum since 1983, helping look for, collect and prepare fossils from across Alberta. He discovered the chemical-preparation method that freed hundreds of three-dimensional glass plant fossils from their matrix, revealing cellular details. Aulenback used the information from these fossils to re-landscape the museum's palaeoconservatory with only modern relatives of plants that lived in the Drumheller area 70 million years ago.

In 1998, Aulenback accompanied Currie to China, where he helped prepare feathered dinosaur fossils.

The Ornithomimus at Home

The *Ornithomimus* found in Dinosaur Provincial Park in 1995 is one of many spectacular dinosaur specimens on display at the Royal Tyrrell Museum of Palaeontology in Drumheller, Alberta.

Located in the heart of the fossil-rich Red Deer River badlands, the museum exhibits the history of life in all its forms and showcases more than 40 complete dinosaurs — one of the largest collections under one roof anywhere. Museum curators study the remains of plants and animals that have lived on our planet through the ages, as well as the fossilized environments they inhabited.

The life-size ornithomimid model on the plaza of the Royal Tyrrell Museum was created by Calgary palaeo-artist Brian Cooley. He incorporated the most recent scientific information known about this group of dinosaurs into the sculpture.

Precambrian Era - birth of the planet
approximately 4.6 billion years ago

Mesozoic Era

Triassic Period (240–185 mya)

Jurassic Period (185–140 mya)